DOOR TO DOOR

Lukas Pharrell

Contents

1. Customer Type #1: The Ones Who Listen To Their Kids 1
2. Customer Type #2: The Ones Who Flirt 10
3. Customer Type #3: The Ones Who Don't Like Your Cause 18
4. Customer Type #4: The Ones Who Don't Answer The Door 29
5. Customer Type #5: The Ones Who Don't Speak English 37
6. Customer Type #6: The Ones Who Tell You Their Life Story 46
7. Customer Type #7: The Ones Who Don't Need Convincing 55
8. Customer Type #8: The Ones Who Are Busy 63
9. Customer Type #9: The Ones Who Are Sceptical 70

10. Customer Type #10: The Ones Who Want The Details 77

Customer Type #1: The Ones Who Listen To Their Kids

"Hello, ma'am, I'm Hudson Ellis - I'm a representative of the charity Man's Best Friend. You may have heard of us?"

The woman raises her eyebrows in a way that clearly indicates she has done no such thing. Hudson takes it as a cue to pull a leaflet out of his bag, holding out to her. "We help disabled dogs," he explains, trying not to let his smile waver when she takes the leaflet but doesn't spare it a second glance.

"Dogs?"

"You know, when they're missing a leg, or blind, or..."

"I know what a disabled dog is," she rolls her eyes. At that precise moment, the small boy who had been hiding behind her legs pokes his head out to study Hudson curiously.

"Do we get a dog if we help you, mister?"

"Well, if your mom decides - "

" – Arthur, you know Daddy doesn't like dogs." The mother gives her son a pointed look. Hudson hesitates, then crouches down to Arthur's level.

"I'll tell you what," he says. "You don't have to take a dog home. But you can still get to take care of one. It's called sponsoring."

"Soponorising?" Arthur repeats, brow furrowing. Hudson nods.

"Exactly. It means you can take care of a dog," he taps the badge pinned to his sweater, which depicts a cartoon dog with three legs jumping to catch a Frisbee, and says I've sponsored a Man's Best Friend! in block letters underneath, "and not have to take it home, so your dad doesn't get upset. If your mom lets you, of course."

Hudson pauses to glance up at the woman, whose gaze seems to have softened considerably. The boy follows suit, staring at his mother with wide, pleading eyes. "Please, Mommy," he tugs at belt loops of her trousers. "Can we please soaparise a doggie?"

She hesitates, pursing her lips. "Alright," she relents. Arthur lets out a whoop. "We're gonna sponosrise a doggie!" he babbles, dancing around the hallway. "A doggie! Of our own!"

Hudson grins, this time with real enthusiasm. "All the information you'll need is in the leaflet with you, ma'am," he tells the woman, who's fighting back a smile of her own at her son's antics (Arthur is now attempting some kind of celebratory cartwheel). "In the meantime if I could just take some form of contact? An email or something would be great, yeah..." he holds out a pen and clipboard, smiling at her when she's done writing on the paper. "Thank you in advance for your help."

“Thank you,” she nods, before stepping away from the doorway – a signal Hudson knows from experience means she’s done talking. He moves the other way, and the door swings shut.

Hudson likes New York, he decides, plodding down the stairs. He likes how there are more pedestrians than taxis and more taxis than big four-by-four cars that take up half the road.

"That's because the only people who own cars in New York are complete assholes," his friend Georgie had told him when he'd first pointed it out. "It's what we have a subway for, dumbass."

After one ride on the subway he already understands what she means - everyone takes it. Old men, young men, teenagers, middle schoolers, pregnant women - pretty much anyone you can think off will be sat on the underground train system, and Hudson finds it really cool. It's interesting to just people-watch on there - after all, these are the people he's going to be trying to convince to help disabled dogs for at least the next few years - he might as well try and remember any New Yorker quirks.

True, the people here might be a little tougher to crack, but they still can be cracked, because so far Hudson's had a 99.9% success rate (the 0.1% was an old man who choked on a walnut halfway through their conversation and shut the door in embarrassment. Hudson waited a few minutes for the guy to open the door again, but he didn't.).

Hudson learnt a long time ago that door-to-door work isn't actually about trying your luck at every door (however many times your employer tries to tell you otherwise) - it's about knowing your customers. If the house has a beach ball and toy slide in its front garden, you should probably try your luck, because a boy like Arthur might just do the convincing of his mom or dad for you. If the house has a rabid dog chained up to its fence, perhaps it's one to skip.

The problem with New York is that they don't have houses - not like in Dallas, anyway. In New York, they all live in apartment blocks, behind doors that all look the same. It means that he has to be more careful, pick his customers after more thought. Even so; 99.9% success rate, so it's all good - and he plans to keep it that way.

☒

"Hello sir, I'm a representative of the charity Man's Best Friend - I was wondering if you had a few spare momen - "

"Man's best friend? As in, dogs?" Hudson smiles at the girl - she looks twelve or thirteen - standing behind the man who answered the door.

"Yep," he nods. "Disabled dogs, actually."

"So what, do we, like, adopt one or sponsor one or something?" the girl asks, clearly taking it upon herself to do all the talking.

"Well, actually, you can choose," Hudson reaches into his bag and chooses to pull out two, handing one to both father and daughter. "If you sponsor one, you'll be giving us the money to help the dog get back on its feet. Then, you can choose to adopt it afterwards. Alternatively, you can just give some money. "

"We should do this, Dad," the girl tells her father, already on the second page of the leaflet by the time Hudson has finished talking.

The man spares his daughter a glance before nodding to Hudson. "I think we'd like to sign up, actually," he nods.

"Great!" Hudson beams and offers the man his clipboard, silently congratulating himself on yet another job well done and thanking God for fathers who were putty in their daughters' hands.

⊠

It's the last flat of his last assigned block of the day (which happens to be directly adjacent to the one he now lives in), and Hudson has to practically heave himself into the elevator, almost dizzy from exhaustion.

The top floor only has one door - Hudson supposes it's some kind of luxury suite-slash-penthouse deal - and he pauses for a second. Unlike most of the other doors in the building, there's not really anything situated on or around it to give him a hint as to whether or not the occupant of the flat is approachable. He shrugs to himself, bringing his knuckles up to the door and rapping them against it, figuring that he might as well take his chances.

After a few moments, a girl who Hudson immediately decides is the most attractive female to walk the earth since Selena Gomez opens the door. Any confidence he might have attempted to instill into himself as part of his pre-knocking ritual is slowly fading away - at the sight of her raised eyebrows and expression of mild distaste it near-vanishes.

"Can I help you?"

With those four words, any remnants of confidence which may have by chance be still left hanging around are thrown into a ditch and trampled upon. Even so, he nods mutely in answer to her question, swallowing and clenching his hand around the strap of his messenger bag.

"I'm - "

"A door-to-door salesman," she leans against the doorway, surveying him in much the same way a shark does its prey. "I'm sorry," she says, sounding the complete opposite as she studies her nails. "But I can guarantee to you that I have absolutely no interest in whatever cheap, unreliable gizmo you have to offer. Or anything you have to offer, period."

Hudson gapes, shocked into speechlessness. She doesn't even glance up.

"Unless it's sex or something similar," she adds lightly as an afterthought, still inspecting her nails. "And even then..." she pauses to give him a pointed once-over. "Well, I would need quite a bit of convincing."

The tips of Hudson's ears go pink in embarrassment, and it takes all of his willpower to prevent his cheeks from following suit. The girl must notice, because he catches the beginnings of a smirk playing at her lips.

"I digress," she continues, still leaning against the doorway. "The point I am trying to make," she skewers him with a look that could most likely burn a hole through a brick wall, "is that I honestly could not care less who you are, or what you are attempting to sell me, and also that I am about to shut this door in your face."

And she does.

Hudson is left standing in silence and staring at a door.

"What the fuck?" he mumbles to himself once he has enough presence of mind to do so. His brain is still trying to process what just occured.

Seven minutes later, and it's still attempting to do - even after he's stumbled into the elevator and then out of the building. He pulls his phone out as he walks home.

Hudson: think i just got burned by the hottest woman on the planet

It only takes a few minutes for his phone to buzz with a response, but he's already in the foyer of his apartment block.

Georgie: it was always going to happen, even your hudson ellis charm wont always work in the big apple

Georgie: but hottest woman?? tell me more

Hudson: i'll call you later

Georgie: you better

He knows he probably looks like a complete idiot, grinning at his phone as he walks into the elevator, but he can't help it. Georgie's just so...Georgie.

She'd most likely punch him for saying that, since it doesn't exactly make sense, but, he tells himself as the elevator lets out a ding and he steps out onto his floor, it's accurate. There isn't an adjective in the dictionary that can accurately describe his best friend.

Hudson fumbles around in his bag, trying to find the keys to his apartment. It takes a little longer than what can be classified as normal - it's only been a day since he moved in, and, as such, he's not even close to being familiar with the shape of his keys.

Another side-effect of recent moving is the boxes everywhere. He's met with some resistance when he finally unlocks the door - after some more pushing he steps inside to find that he somehow managed to place a large cardboard box directly in front of it. After shoving it somewhere where it can't prevent him from actually entering the flat again, Hudson wades through the other boxes into the living space, and grimaces.

There's one reason and one reason only that this apartment has the lowest rent in the entire area: the windows.

Huge, floor-to-ceiling windows that span the entire room and aren't covered by curtains or blinds or anything.

To make matters worse, Hudson has a very direct view into the next apartment over - a view which, of course, goes both ways. He doesn't know who his new neighbour is yet, but judging by the lights that are on, it seems that they're home. He prays to anything and everything that they are at least male.

The neighbour chooses that precise moment to walk into their living space, reading as a book as they walk. Hudson's eyes widen, and he instinctively drops behind some boxes to avoid being seen.

His neighbour is most definitely not male.

Painfully slowly, he moves his head by a fraction of an inch to catch a glimpse of the woman, only to fall backwards with a crash into the boxes behind him.

His neighbour isn't just female - she's the most attractive female to walk the earth since Selena Gomez. The one who slammed a door in his face approximately half an hour ago.

Ah, shit, Hudson thinks.

Customer Type #2: The Ones Who Flirt

"Hello, ma'am, I'm Hudson Ellis - I'm a representative of the charity Man's Best Friend. You may have heard of us?"

"Uh, yeah, I think I might have, actually," the girl looks around his age, maybe a little younger. She flashes him a wide smile as she twirls a strand of her blonde hair around one finger.

"Oh, cool, so you know what it's about," Hudson smiles, reaching for the flap of his bag.

"Don't you help...cats? Or something?"

Hudson purses his lips for a brief second, but immediately returns to his smile, taking out a flyer and handing it to her. "You're close," he tells her, even though she isn't really. "We actually help disabled dogs."

"Oh," she lets out a high pitched laugh that almost grates at Hudson's nerves. "I'm sorry, I must've got them mixed up or something..."

"Easy mistake to make," he assures her, even if though it isn't really. "Anyway, we help disabled dogs, and we have several programmes that you can contribute to - "

"Like sponsoring," the girl taps on the badge pinned to his lapel, and smiles, letting her hand linger on his chest a little too long.

She looks pleased with herself for noticing, and Hudson doesn't want to rain on her parade. "Exactly," he nods, still smiling even though he feels increasingly uncomfortable. "So you can sign up to sponsor one, adopt one, or just donate some money," he punctuates his last suggestion with a shake of the bucket in his right hand - it's already beginning to fill up and it isn't even midday.

"Oh, well, in that case," she fishes into her pocket and brings out a few dollar bills as well as some coins, taking Hudson's hand and dropping the change into it. He resists the urge to jerk it away, instead letting his smile widen. "Thank you so much, miss," he tells her, putting the money into the bucket. "Honestly, your contribution is so useful."

"Is that what you say to all the girls?" Hudson doesn't like the look of the smirk on her face; he subconsciously takes a few steps back and forces a laugh.

"Ha, not really...I just moved here, actually..."

"Oh?" It seems that for every step he takes backwards the girl takes around five forwards. Either way, he doesn't really like their close proximity. "Where are you from, then? Is that a Texas accent I catch?"

"Yep," he lets out another stuttering laugh. "I'm from Dallas."

"Hm, a cowboy."

"I should really - go..."

"Alright, cowboy," she rests a hand on his arm, and Hudson shifts uncomfortably. "But I'd check that bucket of yours. You might find something you didn't count on getting."

He thinks she knows what she's talking about.

"Alright," he tries to smile again, but he's pretty sure it looks more like a grimace. "Thank you again!"

"No problem!"

Once he's halfway down the street, Hudson let's out a breath he didn't realise he'd been holding, pausing to glance ruefully down at the bucket in his hand. Sure enough, he can catch sight of a slip of paper among the green bills - closer inspection reveals a series of numbers that Hudson definitely won't be calling scribbled onto it. He marvels at how she even managed to get the number written and on the slip by the time she'd donated.

⊠

"Hi, sir, I'm - "

"Are you gay?"

Hudson blinks, taken aback. "I..."

"It's okay if you are," the man tells him. "I mean, actually, it's more than okay - "

"I can't say I am, sir," Hudson is sure that he looks and sounds just as confused as he feels. What has his sexuality got to do with anything?

"Right," the man says, before nodding vigorously. "I mean, it was just, you know, a question...not many straight men - "

"You'd be surprised," he offers.

"Yes," the man hesitates before agreeing, nodding again. "Right. Absolutely. Well, sorry, but I don't think I'm actually very interested in you - I mean, what you have to sell, that is..."

Hudson blinks again. Wait, what?

"Sorry, I..." the guy steps back to close the door. Hudson doesn't even have the presence of mind to protest, still very, very confused.

☒

Hudson Ellis updated his status: "Think I just got rejected by a gay guy for...not being gay."

☒

Hudson is on what is effectively his lunch break, at while it's a relief to not be going round knocking on people's doors, he doesn't actually know what to do or where to go. Georgie's off being a book editor and doing whatever it is book editors do, and without her he's pretty much lost, considering he's in a city he just moved into around four days ago.

A huge city he just moved into a few days ago.

Hudson: anywhere i can go for lunch??

Georgie: somewhere where i can't run into you

Hudson: haha

Hudson: no but seriously

Georgie: i am serious

Georgie: i'm always serious

Georgie: go out and explOOOORE

Georgie: just avoid running into me whilst doing so

☒

Hudson only has twenty minutes left of his break, and he's still struggling to find somewhere to eat, considering the first seven places he came across were all various fast food chains, none of which Hudson really cared to step into.

By now, however, he is seriously considering forgoing healthy food and buying himself a Big Mac, because it's one in the afternoon and all he had for breakfast was an apple.

Hudson sighs, and is turning to retrace his steps back to the nondescript McDonalds branch around a block and a half back, when he catches sight of a sixties-style diner, tucked in between an estate agents' and accounting building.

Thank God, he thinks.

☒

It isn't difficult to fall in love with the diner, especially when its servings are plentiful and the burgers taste fucking good. Hudson has to wolf it down so that he isn't late, and he thinks he can catch the cook smiling with amusement, but that's okay.

(He likes making people smile, anyway.)

"You from around here?" the waitress asks with a little too much interest, handing him the bill.

"Uh, no, actually," he replies, tempted to lie but realising it wouldn't go far, because he's clearly not a native. "I'm from Texas."

The waitress' eyebrows go up a little, but her mouth quirks into a smile. "So what's brought you here?"

Hudson shrugs. "Work. Same as most, I guess."

"Hm," she hums in agreement. "Well, hope you make a habit of comin' here...?"

"Uh, Hudson," he provides.

"Hudson," she repeats thoughtfully. "Hope to see you around. And if you ever need any help getting round the city..."

"Oh," his eyes widen with the realisation of her implication. "Right. Thanks."

He considers mentioning Georgie to put her off, but has a distinct feeling that that would somehow backfire, so refrains from doing so. Instead, he glances at his watch (for lack of anywhere else to glance), grimacing at the time.

"I should probably...go..."

"Right," she nods. "Here's your change, Hudson," she pauses, then adds, "I'm Beth. By the way. Just saying."

Hudson bites back a smile - her awkwardness is endearing. "Thanks, Beth," he says sincerely. "I might take you up on that offer of a tour of the city," he tells her at the door.

He leaves and pretends not to hear the muffled "Yes!" emmitted once he's vacated the building.

⊠

Even after he's finished work for the day, Hudson wonders absently if he's giving Beth the wrong idea. He isn't really looking for anything, he considers as he unlocks the door to his apartment. He'd rather not get caught up in something like that, anyway - it's only been, what? Three, four days?Three, he decides, heading straight for the couch and collapsing onto it with a sigh. It's only been three days.

He didn't come to New York for girls - he came for the charity and for living, because New York is one of those cities that makes you feel alive; more alive than he did in Dallas, anyway.

He's distracted from his thoughts by the sight of lights flickering on registering in his peripheral vision. Hudson turns slightly and sees his neighbour kick off her high heels before collapsing onto the couch in much the same manner as he had done only a few minutes before. He watches her turn on the television, and shifts in discomfort before averting his eyes and doing the same. It's ridiculous, he thinks that they can just see into each other's apartments. Isn't there some kind of law against that, or something?

Hudon keeps switching through the channels, more focused on resisting the urge to look back through the windows than actually finding something to watch. He decides there and then that he hates floor-to-ceiling windows and they are the most stupid, pointless thing in existence, right up there with juggling and ties and boasting about how good you are at eating spicy food.

I hate everything, he thinks loudly to himself over the SpongeBob Squarepants theme tune (Why is it even on this late in the evening?)

Eventually, he gives in to the temptation, casting what he hopes is a furtive glance at the opposite apartment as he walks to the kitchen area to grab a snack. His own eyes are met by two green ones, and he trips over a stray cardboard box in surprise, catching himself against the kitchen counter just before he becomes very well-acquainted with the floor. He hastens to look back at her.

What should I do? Oh God, what do I do what should I do oh God oh God oh God -

Before he can second-guess himself, he smiles hesitantly, raising one hand in greeting. A few seconds pass, but she doesn't respond in kind - instead, she sends him a glare that he's pretty sure could probably kill him, even through two layers of glass and brick and whatever else, then turns and leaves the room.

I tried, Hudson tells himself miserably. He isn't sure how he's meant to co-exist with a person who is somehow able to hate him without even knowing his name.

Customer Type #3: The Ones Who Don't Like Your Cause

"Hello, ma'am, I'm Hudson Ellis - I'm a representative of the charity Man's Best Friend. You may have heard of us?"

The woman looks unimpressed. "No."

Hudson blinks. Okay, then. "Well, we're a charity that helps disabled dogs - "

"I'm allergic to dogs," she cuts him off.

"Right, well..." he trails off. "I mean, you don't have to let that stop you, right? If - "

"I'm sorry," the woman interrupts him again, not looking very sorry at all, "I'm not all that interested in helping animals that force me to stick an EpiPen in my thigh and then go to hospital."

There is an awkward silence.

"I'm sure that if you just heard me out - " Hudson begins weakly.

"I'd rather not," she purses her lips. "But thanks for the offer," she adds, as though going for some type of consolation.

Hudson watches the door swing shut. "That went well," he mumbles to himself, still standing in the porch.

☒

"Good morning, sir, I'm - "

"Daddy!"

"Dad!"

"Bert won't give back my tiara - "

"Laura took my Transformers - "

"Dad, Alex is stuck up the tree! Again! And she's going to fall soon!"

The man who opens the door looks very distressed, with a baby cradled in one arm, a small child clinging to his leg, and a plethora of voices emanating from various places in the house behind him.

"Could you be quick?" he asks Hudson desperately. "If Alex has got herself stuck up the tree, I gotta - "

"Um, sure," Hudson nods. "I'm a volunteer for a charity that helps disabled dogs - "

"Oh, Jesus," half of him retains the frantic air, but the other seems close to rolling its eyes. "Could you not be a volunteer for something a little more important? One that helps single dads with five kids, for instance?"

Hudson wonders if it's a joke he should laugh at. Looking over at the man again, he decides it's probably not.

"I understand that - "

"You really don't," the man shakes his head, jogging the baby as he does so. "What are you, twenty, twenty-one?"

"I - "

"Here's some advice for you, kid," he says breathlessly as the shrieks in the house continue, "don't get married. It's not worth it."

"Right," Hudson feels that he's steadily losing a customer. "I really think it would be great if you could consider - "

At that precise moment, the baby in the man's arms chooses to let out a wail that Hudson is pretty sure can be heard from ten blocks away.

The man swears under his breath, already starting to jog the child up and down in an attempt to make it stop crying. Soon enough, the toddler at his feet takes up the cry, both of them bawling in unison.

"Look, kid, I'm sorry, but I got five freaking kids, I don't need a blind dog to add to my troubles," he says briskly over his children's cries.

Hudson considers pointing out the sponsoring programme, but gets the distinct feeling that it wouldn't be received well. Sure enough, he soon finds himself nose-to-nose with a door.

☒

"Hello?"

"Hey, Georgie," Hudson holds the phone to his ear as he crosses the road. "Wanna have lunch?"

"Hm," she hums in consideration. "Guess I could. Considering I haven't seen you since the day I helped you move in."

"Great," Hudson smiles. "I've found this really awesome place, I'll text you where it is."

"As long as you're paying."

"Right," he rolls his eyes.

"Don't roll your eyes."

Hudson splutters. The whole advantage of phone calls has always been that the other person can't see what you're doing, but it seemingly doesn't apply to Georgie. "I wasn't - "

"Yes, you were," she cuts him off. "Text me the address. I'll meet you, like, ten minutes?"

"Sounds good."

"See ya, loser."

"Bye, Georgie."

☒

"So how're the floor-to-ceiling windows working out for ya?" Georgie asks between slurps of a strawberry milkshake.

Hudson doesn't reply, choosing instead to shrug and take a bite out of his burger. Georgie's eyes narrow immediately.

"Okay, spill. There is something up. It's a girl, isn't it?" Her eyes widen. "A hot girl!" she exclaims.

"No!" Hudson protests. "Okay, well, she is hot," he amends at Georgie's raised eyebrows. "But that's not it."

"So what is it, Lover Boy? I think you should take advantage of this, to be honest, I mean you two are clearly going to be very exposed to each other, so you might as well just - "

"Georgie, shut up," Hudson rolls his eyes. "I'm trying to tell you something?"

"Right, right," she waves a hand at him for him to go on.

"So remember when I told you about that girl who basically burned me on my first day of work?"

"Oh my God," Georgie breathes, connecting the dots. "Are you kidding me?"

"No," he says miserably.

"That's - "

"Yes," he says, still miserable.

"She's - "

"Yep."

"But - "

"I know."

"And she - ?"

"Mhm."

"Oh my God."

Hudson sighs. "Basically."

"This is - " Georgie's interrupted by her phone buzzing on the table. She gives Hudson an apologetic look, but he merely waves at her, silently telling her to take the call.

"Hello? Yeah, I..." she gets up and walks away and out of earshot, continuing her conversation. Hudson is left alone to finish his burger.

"Hey, Hudson."

He blinks, pulled out of his thoughts to see a smiling Beth standing over him. "Oh. Hey, Beth."

"So, you liked us enough to come back?" she grins.

"Oh, yeah," he nods eagerly. "This place is great. I'm probably gonna be a regular. Just a heads-up."

"Yeah, I can guess," she laughs. "So who's that girl with you?"

"Oh, Georgie? She's my friend. Well, best friend, actually," he corrects thoughtfully. "She'd probably kill me if I said she was just my friend."

"Right," Beth nods. "So...got any room in the friends department for one more?"

Hudson stares for a moment, not quite understanding her question. She frowns.

"Uh, Hudson?"

"Huh? I mean, yeah! Of course!" he replies quickly, nodding a little too frantically. "Definitely!"

She raises an eyebrow. "Are you okay...?"

He opens his mouth to reply, but is cut off by Georgie, who has returned to the booth with a doleful expression on her face.

"Bad news," she says in a regretful tone of voice. "Looks like I have to go straight back to work because some dickhea - oh," she blinks at Beth, as though seeing her for the first time. "Hudson...? Is this a...friend? Of yours?"

"Uh, yeah," he replies. "Georgie, Beth. Beth, Georgie."

"Hi," Georgie says warmly, jutting out her hand for Beth to shake. "You guys make really good food. Seriously."

"Thanks," Beth smiles.

"But I kind of need to leave now," Georgie grabs her coat from the booth. "I'll call you," she tells Hudson, already moving towards the exit.

"Okay," Hudson says. "See ya. Don't work too hard."

"I won't!" she calls, then the sound of the door opening and closing signals her exit.

"She seems nice," Beth comments.

"Oh, she is, until you get to know her," Hudson replies in a droll tone of voice. She laughs at his sarcasm.

"Nice to see you think highly of her."

"Oh, I do," he assures her. "But don't tell her I said that," he adds as an afterthought.

"My lips are sealed," Beth tells him.

"Good," he smiles. "So, about that tour - "

"Beth! Stop chatting up the customers and come back to work!"

"I'm coming!" she calls. "I'll talk to you later," she tells Hudson. He nods.

Beth goes back to the counter, and he sits in silence finishing his milkshake (and Georgie's), before his attention is attracted by the door opening and closing and of all the people that could've walked in, it just has his floor-to-ceiling buddy.

Hudson watches her order her food briskly, and even though she's on the other side of the room, he can tell her tone is business-like. He's surprised, however, when he can make out her sending a small smile to Beth as she notes down her order.

The woman has a sort of air about her that screams the word power. Her hair is a deep chestnut and curls slightly at the edges, and she has eyes to match. Her skin is tan enough to border on brown and betray some kind of Cherokee heritage - or so Hudson thinks, anyway - and her smile flickers; there one moment, gone the next. Hudson doesn't know shit about fashion, but he can tell that she knows what she's doing - her outfit is perfectly put together.

He stares at her until she leaves with her takeaway. He keeps staring at the door until Beth flicks his arm.

"Ow!" he protests, rubbing the area in question.

"You were unresponsive," she says by way of explanation.

"Who's that woman you were just serving?" Hudson asks her abruptly.

"You mean Piper?" Beth frowns.

"I...yeah," he nods.

She shrugs. "Well, she's...Piper, I guess. She's the head editor of some fashion magazine. She scares people shitless, but she's actually pretty cool, when you get to know her," she tells him. "Actually, come to think of it, she never leaves this place without tipping. And she tips good."

"Right," Hudson says absently.

"Why, you like her?" Beth nudges him with a wicked grin.

"Nah," he shakes his head, unable to keep a matching smile from spreading across his face.

"Aw, you so do!" she cries, pinching his cheeks. "Look at you, with your lil' cheeks and lil' smile - "

"Stop it," he slaps her hands away and rolls his eyes, but it's less effective when he has a wide grin on his face.

"Talk to her next time you come in," Beth advises, still grinning. "Maybe she'll - "

"Beth! Get your ass back on the job!"

☒

"Hi, sir," Hudson smiles pleasantly at the middle-aged man who opens the door. "I'm - "

"Who is it, honey?" a woman who looks about the man's age joins him in the doorway. "Oh. Hello."

"Hello," he aims for another warm smile. "I'm Hudson Ellis, I'm a representative for the charity Man's Best Friend."

"As in, dogs?"

"Yep," he nods, still smiling. "We actually help disabled dogs - "

"Oh, no, son," the man interrupts, shaking his head. "Disabled dogs should be put down."

"I - what?"

"Hm," the woman, to Hudson's amazement, nods in agreement. "Better to put them out of their misery."

"But - " Hudson says, almost indignant. "They don't need to be in misery, if we can just get them help first - "

"No point in tryingta fix what's already broken," the man shrugs.

"That's like saying we should kill off kids that are born with disabilities!" Hudson exclaims, unable to stop himself from breaking the customer is always right policy.

"But these aren't kids, honey, they're dogs," the woman reminds him with a condescending smile. "Now, honestly, are you trying to tell me there isn't a big difference between the two?"

Hudson pauses to stare, open-mouthed, at the couple, gaze shifting from the man to the woman and back.

"I see," he says after some time, an edge to his voice. "I guess this charity isn't for you."

"Guess not," the man says lightly, shrugging.

"Thank you for your time," Hudson says coldly. Then, for the first time since he's arrived in New York, he walks away from the house before they close the door.

⊠

Hudson's in a bad mood by the time he gets home, and seeing Piper already in her flat and cooking herself dinner somehow doesn't help things. There's something about her that makes him feel incredibly stupid.

(Well, something apart from the vivid memory of her making him sound incredibly stupid, then slamming the door of her flat in his face. But he's trying to let that go.)

When he enters the apartment, he thinks he catches her eyes slant towards the windows slightly, but they return to her chicken-frying just as quickly, and she somehow doesn't spare him or his apartment a second glance for the rest of the evening. Hudson considers writing his name on a piece of paper and pressing it to the window - almost just to see how she would respond. But before he can even think about it, she's gone - grabbing her laptop from the kitchen island and disappearing into another room.

Customer Type #4: The Ones Who Don't Answer The Door

"Hello, ma'am, I'm Hudson Ellis - I'm a representative of the charity Man's Best Friend. You may have heard of us?"

"Oh, yeah," the woman looks around Hudson's age, maybe a little older, with deep red hair, warm brown eyes, and a smattering of freckles across her nose. Hooped earrings dangle from her ears, and she's wearing many bright colours her outfit practically blinds Hudson. "We're actually already signed up to your sponsoring programme. Have been for a few years now. Right, Brett?"

She glances back at the tall, lean man who has come up to stand behind her. He nods in confirmation, pushing up his glasses when they fall slightly from the movement.

"Oh," Hudson lets the monosyllable fall off his lips in surprise. Hastily, he reaches for the laminated diagram in his bag, scanning it for the small rectangle representing Brett and the woman's house.

Sure enough, it's coloured a flurorescent green, indicating that the occupants have already contibuted to the charity.

"I'm so sorry," he tells the both of them earnestly. "I honestly didn't realise..."

The woman's eyes are made even warmer with amusement, and she bites her lip to suppress a grin from blooming onto her face. "Don't sweat it," she tells him.

Brett nods again, his smile matching the woman's. "You're only human, Mister Hudson Ellis," he says, tone made light with humour.

Trying not to look too surprised at his recollection of his name, Hudson smiles. "Right," he steps away from the porch, still smiling. "I'm sorry for wasting your time, sir, ma'am."

"Aw man, don't call me that, I feel old," she chastises him. "I'm Rachel. Just Rachel."

"And I'm Just Brett," Brett jokes.

"Sorry," Hudson apologises. "Rachel. Brett."

"Better," she tells him, lips quirking up into another smile. "But we should probably let you get back to your job now. Have an awesome morning, Hudson."

"You too," he murmurs as the door swings shut.

God, he loves nice people.

⊠

Hudson tugs himself up the last flight of stairs of the apartment block, pausing to take a few deep breaths, bent over with his hands braced on his thighs.

(Why does he get the distinct feeling that since coming to New York and discovering that goddamn diner he's gotten a little...unfit?)

"Okay," he breathes aloud, straightening up, chest still heaving. "I'm okay."

He makes his way to first of the two doors on the top floor, pausing once more to catch his breath (again), before knocking.

There is no response.

"You have got to be shitting me," Hudson mutters under his breath. He did not come all this way only for the residents of the flat to be out.

Praying to all that is good and holy, he brings his knuckles to the wood once more, rapping slightly louder this time.

Still no response.

"You know what?" he says aloud to no one in particular. "I'm over it. I am fucking over it." He huffs, grabbing a leaflet from his bag and shoving it under the door. Turning and glancing at the other door, Hudson considers knocking, but realises his ego could not take another blow if the residents of that flat also happened to be out.

"I hate everything," he sighs as he begins his descent.

☒

"Hey, Hudson!" Beth grins at him, the corners of her eyes crinkling slightly. Hudson beams back. "The usual?" she asks.

He's about to nod, before remembering the pain he went through just to try and climb a few flights of stairs that morning. "Actually, I think I'll just have a salad," he tells her. Beth raises her eyebrows.

"A salad? You want a salad?"

"Nothing wrong with a change," Hudson says weakly.

She studies him for a moment, before shrugging. "Alright," she concedes, scribbling down his order. "But Jesse isn't gonna be happy. He's already got your burger on the grill."

Hudson feels an unexpected rush of warmth course through him at the words. "He has?"

"Uh huh," Beth nods, then adds, with a wry smile, "I'll tell him to pack it up for you to take home."

"No, you don't - "

"Hudson, do you have anybody at home who knows how to cook a decent meal?"

"I..." he trails off. When she put it that way...

"I thought so," Beth looks triumphant. "I'll tell him to pack it up for you to take home," she repeats. This time, Hudson doesn't protest , instead giving her a grateful look.

"One salad coming right up," she tells him, moving away. He smiles and leans into the seat of the booth, the rush of warmth still lingering within him. If he closes his eyes, he almost feels...at home. Like less of a stranger and more of someone who belongs here.

The bell of the shop door tings. Out of force of habit, Hudson's eyes stray towards the door, but he doesn't feel a surge of surprise at the sight of Piper stepping into the diner.

(She's too much of a regular and so is he. He wonders absently if she's noticed him yet. He's always made a habit of sitting in a booth near the back, so maybe not.)

What does invoke a stir of interest is Piper choosing not to take her lunch in a paper bag and walk straight back out of the door, but instead going to sit down at a table, taking out a leatherbound planner and beginning to scribble in it.

"Hm," Hudson hums to himself, trying to keep himself from watching her too closely. Her hair swings prettily across her face, falling just shy of her shoulders, but enough for Hudson not to actually see her - which is perhaps for the best, since him and Piper don't exactly have a great track record.

Him and Piper. He snorts to himself. As if there's a him and Piper.

A small, whimsical part of him debates just going over and sitting down next to her, even though he knows it is something that will never happen. Hi, he would say. You probably want to cut off my balls just for sitting ten yards within your near vicinity, but since we can see into each other's flats pretty much twenty-four seven, and the landlord is a dick and won't let me put up curtains, perhaps we should get to know each other a little better. Because I like to not have to dress fully first thing in the morning just to go out and make myself some breakfast. A guy needs some quality time with his boxers, y'know? And I'm sure you...okay, well...maybe...never mind...

I even manage to screw up in my mind, Hudson thinks ruefully, pursing his lips. His own awkwardness notwithstanding, he would like to know Piper better, and not just because she's really, really attractive. He thinks it would be nice to do stupid things like write each other notes and press them up against the window, or communicate with sign language, or come up with a whole new code they could use that involves flashlights. It's stupid, but he lives for the stupid things.

Although somehow, he doubts that she does too.

"One salad," a waitress who isn't Beth slides his dish onto the table. "With added fried chicken chunks and extra mayonnaise."

Hudson frowns. "But I didn't ask for added- "

"Compliments of the chef," the waitress cuts him off, grinning. Hudson looks up to find Jesse smiling in their direction, giving Hudson a salute with his spatula when they make eye contact."

"That's real nice of you guys," Hudson says quietly with a small smile. "Thank you."

"No prob, Hudson," the waitress smiles. "Anything for our favourite regular." And yeah, okay, that makes Hudson grin like an idiot.

☒

Hudson is on a metaphorical high when he rings the doorbell of his next prospective customer, having garnered sixteen donations and seven sponsorships in the past half hour. His track record is ruined, however, when he presses the small button of the doorbell for the third time and the door fails to be opened.

Shrugging, he slots a leaflet through the letterbox of the porch door, hesitates, then grabs a start-up pack out of his bag, deciding to add it in for good measure.

Logic has never been Hudson's strong point. Most people would've realise that a pack of that particular size would not have fit through said letterbox, no matter how much shoving was involved.

Logic has never been Hudson's strong point.

"Fit - through - the - damn - hole - god - damnit - !" he chokes out through gritted teeth, leaning his entire weight against the door as he tries to fit the pack through the damn hole.

Then, the burglar alarm goes off.

"Shit!" he shouts over the shrill squealing of the alarm, letting the pack slip through his fingers. "Shit shit shit shit shit!" Hudson makes a beeline for the the road, running through the front garden and vaulting over the low fence, not even bothering to go through the gate. A small voice in the back of his head points out that he'll look even more like an actual burglar now, but most of him is completely focused on distancing himself as far as possible from the house whose alarm he has set off, letting his feet move with a speed he didn't know he had through random streets until he can only hear the high pitched screeching as an echo in his head.

"Oh my God," he manages through stuttering breaths as he leans against a random building. "Oh my God."

Hudson is never leaving start-up packages at doors again.

⊠

Piper is already home when Hudson enters his flat - a bit of a change, since she actually usually finishes later than him. She sits cross-legged on her couch, typing at her laptop. She seems so fixated on what she's doing that she doesn't even notice him come into his own apartment, something that Hudson thinks to himself is probably for the best, considering post I-set-off-the-burglar-alarm-in-someone's-house-but-I'm-not-a-burglar-but-I-ran-away-anyway is most likely not the best look on him.

In fact, Hudson considers as he stretches out with a yawn. It's late.

(Okay, it's eight thirty. Not the point.)

He'll just go to sleep now, he decides. He can have the burger they gave him at the diner this afternoon for breakfast. Or something. Either way, he's not in the mood to spend his night in the complete view of Piper, scary hot attractive girl wonder.

Blinking with tired eyes, he gives her another glance - she's still completely focused on her laptop. Before he can convince himself that it's a bad idea, he grabs a random notebook from the coffee table and a large blue marker, then scribbles something onto the paper. Casting around for some sellotape, he finds some, then presses the paper to his window and taping it on. Piper doesn't look up, but he figures she'll see it eventually. He yawns, thinks about he wrote, tells himself that it's good enough, then heads for his bedroom.

Hi. I'm Hudson (your neighbour). How 'bout these windows, huh?

Customer Type #5: The Ones Who Don't Speak English

"Hello, ma'am, I'm Hudson Ellis - I'm a representative of the charity Man's Best Friend. You may have heard of us?"

"Ah ... ein weiterer Verkäufer. Warum ist das hier legal?"

Hudson blinks. He doesn't speak German, but he gets the sense that her muttered words weren't for him. "Uh...we help disabled dogs," he offers weakly.

"Hunde?"

He doesn't know what a hunde is, but hoping that it's a German word for disabled dogs, he nods hesitantly. "Yeah. Uh...hunde."

"Dieser Junge klingt blöd," the woman murmurs under her breath. Hudson stamps down the urge to panic and run away.

"Anyway..." he clears his throat. "I was wondering if you'd be interested in helping our charity?"

"Dies ist eine Wohltätigkeitsorganisation?" the woman asks, eyes widening with what Hudson really hopes is understanding, because at least one of them would actually know what the hell is going on.

"Uh..." the desire to flee has now mulitplied tenfold.

The woman rolls her eyes. "You...charity?"

He almost cries in relief. English. True, broken English, but English. "Yes," he nods, "for dogs."

"Dogs. Hunde," she tells him. "In Deutsch."

"Oh," Hudson feels like his nod to comprehension ratio is currently a little uneven. "I see."

"I help," she nods at the clipboard in Hudson's hand, and thank God. "Sign?"

"Yes," he says a little too quickly. "I mean...please." A thought occurs to him as she writes her contact.

"Danke...?" he says hesitantly as she draws away. The woman lets out a laugh, and Hudson feels his insides warm up a little.

"Gern geschehen."

⊠

"You're lucky I'm here to come over and make sure you don't die from malnutrition," Georgie tells him as she slides a salmon fillet onto her plate and then another onto his. "For just how long do you plan on living on Top Ramen alone?"

Hudson shrugs, already preoccupied with his dinner. Georgie rolls her eyes, but follows his example and begins cutting up her salmon. "Remind me how you got through college?" she asks before popping a forkful into her mouth.

"Roommate was minoring in culinary arts," Hudson mumbles around a mouthful of salmon. "This is so good."

"Oh yeah, what happened to him? And I know it is."

"I don't know," Hudson says thoughtfully. "I should probably call him up."

"I agree," Georgie says, swallowing another bite. "You need all the friends you can get."

"Hey!"

"I speak only the truth," she smirks.

"Shut up," he flicks a piece of broccoli at her from across the table.

"Oh, mature, Hudson, real mature," Georgie says with mild disgust as she picks it off her sleeve.

"You love me," he tells her, returning to his salmon.

"God knows why," she mutters, but bites back a smile as she does so. They spend a few minutes in comfortabl silence, before Georgie breaks it. "Alright, are you going to tell me what that is or am I going to have to guess?"

Hudson frowns in confusion; in response, Georgie nods to the piece of paper taped to the window.

"Oh," Hudson says eloquently. Georgie raises her eyebrows. "Uh huh," she says. "You better start talking, Lover Boy."

"Geez, Georgie, are you ever gonna lay off with the nicknames?" Hudson tries to put it off, but she sees right through him.

"Spill."

"It's no big deal," he protests. "I just thought I'd say hi."

"So instead of going over and knocking on the door like a normal person, you tape notes to the window?"

"Oh, you know what, you're right, Georgie, I should totally go and knock on her door and see what happens, considering my track record with her in that department," he snaps in response.

Georgie is silent for a moment, then her face breaks out into a wide grin. "What?" Hudson growls.

"You really like her, don't you?" Georgie laughs. "Hudson's got a cruuuush - !"

"Georgie, shut up," Hudson hisses, because he doesn't know yet if those floor-to-ceiling windows are soundproof.

"Do you even know her name yet?"

"Yes, actually," he sniffs. "Her name's Piper, and she's head editor of a fashion magazine."

Georgie looks impressed. "So you talked to her?"

Hudson shifts, uncomfortable. "Not exactly..."

The look on his best friend's face is scandalous.

"Oh my God. Hudson Ellis, you complete stalker!"

"Sssh!" he reaches over and puts his hand over her mouth, painfully aware of the fact that Piper has just come into the room.

In sleepwear.

Oh, Jesus God.

Hudson can't help but stare, jaw hanging open slightly, with his hand still clamped across Georgie's mouth and his body halfway across the table. He's pulled out of his trance by a hard kick to the shin administered by Georgie, who scowls once he has enough presence of mind to unlatch his hand from her lips and return to his seat.

"I'd prefer if you didn't get a hard-on whilst we're having dinner," she deadpans. Hudson feels the tips of his ears get warmer and crosses and uncrosses his legs in a valiant attempt to get rid of the aforementioned hard-on.

"She's hot," he mumbles under his breath by way of explanation, barely loud enough for Georgie to hear.

"I'll give you that," Georgie says in a fair-enough tone of voice. He looks up to find her studying Piper discreetly.

"Hey! So I'm not allowed to look but you are?" he whines.

"I never said you weren't allowed to look," she argues, still surveying Piper (who, to Hudson's chagrin, is now bending over to retrieve something beyond his view. Just when he thought any uncomfortable visits from his little buddy were finally off the cards). "I just don't want to have to pretend that I can't see your hard-on. And by that, I mean that I don't want there to be a hard-on at all."

"Gotcha," Hudson mutters, having the decency to look embarrassed.

"Looks like she's noticed your little message," Georgie observes. Hudson whips around so quickly he's pretty sure he hears a few of the muscles in his neck click. Sure enough, Piper is looking up at the piece of paper on the glass, a frown of confusion on her face that Hudson quickly decides is one of the most adorable things he's ever seen. There's a brief moment during which he thinks that she might, well, do something, but alas – she merely stares at it a little longer, before shaking her head, running her hands through her hair (and wow okay that is an image Hudson is mentally saving for eternity and possibly a little longer than that), and exiting the room, revered laptop in hand.

There is a moment of silence.

"Well, that was an anti-climax," Georgie says, standing up and stretching. "You're clearing the table. Since I fed you and all."

⊠

"Morning, sir, I'm a representative for Man's Best Friend, we help –"

"¿Tu eres policía?" The man looks very concerned. Hudson resists the urge to groan and tries to recall what little Spanish he can from high school lessons he didn't pay very much attention to.

"Uh...no? Soy..." he trails off. Great. Already falling at the first hurdle, he thinks to himself.

"¿Tú no eres policía?" The man looks a little more hopeful. Hudson doesn't see the use in letting him down.

"Yes...?"

The man goes back to looking borderline terrified. Ah, shit, Hudson thinks. "¿Está la policía o no?" the man asks in a tone that implies finality. Hudson's glad. At least someone is sure.

"No," he says, figuring he has a fifty-fifty chance of getting somewhere with this man depending on whether he says yes or no. It seems he's made the right choice, because now the man looks a lot more relaxed, and fishes a leaflet out of his back pocket.

"You want tacos?"

Hudson blinks. "Um...no," he hesitates, scrabbling around for the word for thank you in his memory. "Gracias," he blurts out when it comes to him in a sudden burst of enlightenment. "No. Gracias."

The man gives a shrug which is clearly a suit yourself and fuck you all rolled together in one that Hudson doesn't need to know Spanish to understand. He clears his throat, before reaching into his leaflet and pulling out a leaflet of his own, hoping the pictures inside will be able to illustrate what his less than adequate Spanish skills cannot.

This was not in the job description, he thinks to himself ruefully. "Uh...charitia?" he tries, because as every student who has tried to pass a Spanish class without actually working knows, pretty much every English word on the planet sounds more Spanish if one tacks an ia onto the end.

The man raises a critical eyebrow. "Organización benefice," he corrects.

"Right." Hudson bites back a grimace. Oh well, Jesus, if you can so easily understand my amateur's Spanish, how about trying to speak English? he thinks darkly. We aren't in Mexico any more, amigo.

"Organisation benefishe," Hudson points at the leaflet. "For, uh. Perro."

He sincerely hopes that is actually the word for dog and that he's not grimly mistaken.

"Sí," the man nods in what is presumably understanding. "¿Donación?"

Please. "Sí," Hudson nods eagerly. "¿Um...por favor?"

The man snorts. "¿No hablas español, huh?"

Oh, how did you guess? Hudson thinks to himself furiously. Was it my inability to tell you about what I want you to donate money for or the way I fucked up the pronounciation of "sí"?

Instead of voicing these thoughts (although Hudson gets the sense that even if he did, not many of them would be completely understood), Hudson shakes the bucket in his right hand. The man rolls his eyes, before digging into his pocket and throwing a few cents into it.

"Gracias. Señor."

"No hay problema, chico," the man shrugs, looking supremely uninterested. "Bye."

Hudson scowls at the door that is slammed in his face.

☒

There's a note taped to the other window when Hudson gets home.

He scrambles to the window over some stray boxes that haven't yet been cleared away (even though it's been almost a month and a half since he's moved in) to look at it. Piper herself isn't home, but he can still make out the note, the writing on it big but graceful in style.

Gee, you don't know when to quit, do you? I didn't know a person could bounce back from having a door slammed in their face.

It's not much, but it's enough to put a stupid grin on Hudson's face and make his insides feel like chocolate that's been left in the sun too long.

NOTE THAT I WROTE TO MY FOLLOWERS (22.02.16)

hey gang i just have a lil somethin that i wanted to say so here i am.....sayin itbasically i wrote door to door when i was 14 and a complete tosser. and y'all give it a lot of love which i'm always grateful for, but i just wanted to mention a comment that hudson (the main character) makes in ch5 of the book. you can find it pretty easily but the essence is he's talking to a man who doesn't speak english fluently whilst in new york and he makes a catty comment about his ethnicity in his own internal monologue.this was a comment intended to play for laughs, 100%. when i was fourteen i had no idea about how even the smallest things (this is small, really, it's like one sentence) in books can matter so much. i like to think that i've since changed, but it's literally been bugging me for the past three years of my life lol so i thought i'd just get it outthe essence is: i'm sorry for being a shitdick when i was 14. as the daughter of two people who do not have english as their first language, i often rise up in arms about the kinds of comments that my own character made in my own book. i want to clarify that whilst hudson as a character/entity COULD have said something like that, it would only be valid if he was then shown to be wrong and a bit of a dipshit, which he wasn't, and that's what i'm sorry about. he was shown by me writing to be in the right and funny as he does it and that's not cool.so basically, i fucked up. like, three years ago, but it's still there. so i'm sorry. i hope you guys agree that i have significantly more chill now. and that's all.love y'all always,maz

Customer Type #6: The Ones Who Tell You Their Life Story

"Hello, ma'am, I'm Hudson Ellis - I'm a representative of the charity Man's Best Friend. You may have heard of us?"

"Oh," the woman lets out on an exhale. "You're not James," she says simply.

Hudson frowns. "Um, no. Sorry."

"I..." She trails off, and there's a pregnant pause, before her whole body goes limp and she practically collapses into the doorframe. Hudson takes a step forward, concerned, only to take another one when she starts sobbing into the wood. "I'm sorry," she manages, voice muffled, "it's just...I miss him so much, you know?"

"Um," says Hudson. He's not really sure what to tell her. He's never been good with crying girls.

(Or any girls.)

"James is in Afghanistan," she sniffles. Hudson's eyes widen with understanding. "Oh."

"He's meant to be coming home today," she tells him while wiping her eyes - he notes with some relief that she's crying a little less now. "But I just...I don't know. I've got this stupid idea in my head that he won't, you know? That at the last minute I'll get a phone call and..."

To Hudson's dismay, she falls back into a fit of crying. He hesitates for a moment, then reaches a hand out to rest on her shoulder, figuring she can't arrest him for rape on that count.

She surprises him by falling completely into him, still sobbing. Okay, Hudson thinks to himself, awkwardly bringing his hands around to pat her back. Hugs with random strangers are a thing now.

"I'm sure he'll be home before you know it," he manages in what he hopes is a tone that conveys comfort rather than awkwardness or dismay. "I betcha he's getting off that plane right now. He'll come home for you, right?"

"Yeah," she mumbles into his jacket (which, luckily, is waterproof). "You're right." A few more minutes pass before she pulls away, cheeks flushed a pale pink.

"Oh my God," she says in a near-whisper, tone heavy with embarrassment. "You must think I'm some kind of freak, doing...oh God, I'm sorry, I don't know what came over me..."

"It's okay," he says gently.

She opens her mouth, presumably to say something, then closes it and shakes her head. "Here," she says. "You're collecting for a charity, right?"

Hudson nods with a smile. "Charity for disabled dogs," he tells her.

"Oh, wow," her eyes brighten. "My mom and I used to have a blind dog, before I left home to live with James. Hold on," she leaves him at the doorstep, heading into the apartment. She comes back out a few moments later, bearing two fifty dollar bills.

"Wow," Hudson says before he can help it. "I mean, thank you so much," he adds on hastily.

She smiles widely at him. "It's the least I could do," she says, dropping the notes into the bucket. "After spazzing out on you like that."

"Thank you, Miss," he says softly.

"Aubrey," she corrects. "Again, least I could do," her eyes flicker to his name tag. "Hudson."

Then the weirdest thing happens.

She hugs him again. And he hugs her back. Even though she's basically a stranger. And it's nice.

☒

"Hi, sir, I'm a - "

"You what?"

Hudson purses his lips, hesitating as he looks at the old man fiddling with the hearing aid in his ear, trying to recall the protocol for relaying your message to people who are hard of hearing.

A few moments later, and he still can't remember anything – so he abandons training completely (God knows he's been doing a lot of that ever since arriving in New York) and decides to go through the foolproof method: loud and slow.

"I'm a volunteer," Hudson says around forty decibels louder than usual. "For a charity. We help disabled dogs."

"Disabled hogs?"

"Dogs," he increases the volume of his voice a little more. "Disabled dogs."

"Ah," the man nods in understanding. Hudson tries to keep the look of relief from spreading onto his face. "You know, young man, I'm familiar with a lot of disabled dogs."

"Are you?" Hudson asks, deciding to shift to a more comfortable standing position. He recognises the hallmarks of a life story when he sees them, and these are definitely the hallmarks of a life story.

"Damn straight," the man nods. "Dogs won us the war against those Germans, y'know."

"Really?" he replies, although it's probably not necessary. If there's anything longer than a life story, it's a war-related life story.

"Uh huh," the man nods. "Actually, I remember this one time that a dog saved my life, back in forty-one..."

Hudson sighs to himself. This may be some time.

☒

"And bam! I only just made it out alive! And even then, my leg didn't come out with me!" The man lifts his trouser leg up slightly, revealing a prosthetic.

"No way," Hudson gasps. "What about the dog?"

A look of sadness passes across the man's face. "He didn't..."

"Oh," Hudson clears his throat.

In retrospect, he had expected for the old man's story to result in a few minutes of extra Hudson Ellis nap-time (he perfected the art of sleeping whilst standing up with one's eyes open long, long ago). But the mentions of brave sniffer dogs and bombs and biplanes had hooked him in. He's been standing at the old man's doorstep, enraptured, for something close to twenty minutes.

"Anyway," the man claps Hudson's shoulder. "You want some money for this charity of yours," he says whilst dipping his hand into a pocket, presumably looking for some spare change.

"If that's alright by you," Hudson says, a little hesitantly. Sure enough, the sound of metal hitting metal results a few minutes later as the man drops some coins into the bucket.

"Thanks, sir," he tells the old man gratefully.

"No problem, young man. Remember that old story, huh? Maybe you'll tell it to someone."

"Sure," Hudson grins.

⊠

"Hey, Beth," Hudson almost shouts in greeting. The diner is ridiculously busy – it's almost as if all of New York decided to turn up and have lunch at the same time.

"Sorry, Hudson, can't talk now, gotta wait on these tables," she near-yells back, evidently not hearing his original greeting.

He just grins, and casts around for a table to sit, only to stop short when he realises that there aren't any.

"Oh," Beth says of his predicament as she comes to stand next to him, evidently having found a spare moment. "That's awkward."

"It's okay," Hudson shakes his head. "I'll just grab a burger at McDonalds or something – "

"McDonalds," Beth scoffs in disgust. "No way. We'll find you a seat easy."

Hudson is about to point out that that's actually physically impossible, but Beth is already looking in a particular direction, a smile beginning to curve onto her face. He follows her line of sight, only to let his own eyes widen.

Piper is sitting alone at a table with two seats.

"Oh, no way," he says, already shaking his head vehemently. "Beth, no."

Beth already knows about as much as Georgie about Hudson's situation when it comes to Piper (awkward floor-to-ceiling window issues included). In fact, she's pretty much become his closest friend in New York, bar Georgie. Perhaps that's why she grins deviously and presses a hand to the small of his back, pushing him towards the table and ignoring his protests all the while.

"Beth – "

"Hey, Piper," Beth chirps. The woman in question looks up from her food, arching her eyebrow at Beth and Hudson.

"Hi, Beth," she says slowly, eyes narrowing slightly. Hudson can practically feel her beginning to piece things together.

"We're kind of backed up on seats and tables here, obviously," Beth somehow manages to retain her bright tone. Hudson is in awe. He feels very close to pissing himself. "So would you mind sharing your table with Hudson for today?"

Piper's eyes flit to him for barely a second, and he thinks he catches a flicker of recognition in them. "I suppose I can make a concession, for you, Beth," she says wryly, already returning to her food.

"Great! Thanks, Piper!" Beth says happily. "I'll bring your food over here, Hudson."

And then she's gone.

Come back, he feels like calling. Don't leave me here to be ripped to pieces.

"You can sit down, you know," he almost falls over at the sound of her voice. She hasn't even looked up. "I don't bite." There's a pause. "Despite how our first meeting may have given off a different impression," she adds in a pensive tone.

The fact that she's seemingly making it into a joke puts Hudson a little more at ease. He sits down gingerly.

"So," she looks him in the eye, properly, for what Hudson is pretty sure is the first time ever. It makes him feel warm and nervous at the same time. "I never really found out what it was you were trying to sell me that day."

There's a pause, before Hudson realises that this is a roundabout way of starting a conversation. She's having a conversation with me, he thinks, practically elated. Realising she's still expecting an answer, he clears his throat. "I, uh, don't sell anything, actually."

"Oh?"

"I'm with a charity. We help disabled dogs."

She nods, spearing a piece of lettuce with her fork. Hudson tries not to stare as she eats it, because that is creepy and altogether a little too hormonal-teenage-boy to be a good idea.

"Different to what I thought," she acknowledges.

"What did you think?" he blurts out before he can stop himself.

She studies him. "Well, I thought you were a door-to-door salesman," she says carefully. "And an annoying one," she adds. "You had that stupid grin on your face as soon as I opened the door and I thought here we go, another dick to put up with, even on my day off from work, so I suppose I made the executive decision to not allow you to display any dickish qualities and I did that by being dickish myself." Piper pauses, before adding: "and that's as close to an apology as you're ever going to get."

Hudson can't help it, now: he lets the aforementioned stupid grin spread widely onto his face. "Apology accepted," he tells her. Piper rolls her eyes.

"One Hudson burger and fries," Beth has arrived with his food, placing it onto his table and moving away with a knowing smile and a wink. "Enjoy," she says lightly.

(Hudson has a feeling she's not referring to the food.)

"Hudson burger, huh?" Piper has that wry smirk on her face again, and he decides it's one of his favourite facial expressions on the planet (but only on her face).

"I'm a regular," he says by way of explanation, plucking a fry from his plate and popping it into his mouth.

"So am I, I don't see any Piper salads on the menu," she retorts.

Hudson shrugs. “It’s not like that. I’m just really picky when it comes to my burgers. I’m always asking for a shitload of different toppings. So they decided to call in the Hudson burger.”

“I see,” she says with amusement. Hudson tries to save the sound to his memory, figuring it might be the closest he’ll get to a laugh from her (today, at least).

“I’m kinda glad you don’t hate me,” Hudson says after swallowing a bite of burger. “Because this last month has been really awkward and hopefully it’s gonna be less awkward,” he falters, realising he may have come off as a little too confident. “I mean. Maybe. If you want it to be.”

The smirk returns. “We’ll see, Hudson.”

Customer Type #7: The Ones Who Don't Need Convincing

"Hello, ma'am, I'm Hudson Ellis - I'm a representative of the charity Man's Best Friend. You may have heard of us?"

"Uh, sure. You help dogs, right?"

"Yep," Hudson nods, smiling widely. "Disabled dogs."

The woman's eyes soften immediately. "Oh, that's so lovely. Do you want a donation?"

"Actually," Hudson fishes a leaflet out of his bag, opening it and showing it to her. "You can do a few different things. We have an adoption programme," he points to the relevant section of text, "a sponsoring scheme," he moves his finger to the other side of the leaflet. "and like you said, madam, just regular donation," he turns it over and shows her the back.

"Oh, wow," she laughs. "That's a lotta options."

Hudson grins. "It sure is. You're spoilt for choice."

"Hm," she studies the leaflet, which is still in Hudson's outstretched hand. "I think I'll stick with donation for now," she decides. "But if I could keep the leaflet, and think about some of the others as well..."

"Oh, sure, of course," Hudson nods eagerly. "Actually, I think I have an introductory pack with me..." He pauses to dig around in his bag, retrieving said pack and holding it out to her. "It just tells you about the sponsoring and adoption in a little more detail," he explains as she takes it from him.

"Great," she smiles, reaching over to drop a ten dollar bill into Hudson's bucket.

"Thank you," Hudson says, smiling.

"No problem," she smiles back as she moves to close the door.

"Have a good day!" Hudson says, taking a few steps back.

"You too!"

⊠

"Hey, Jesse," Hudson greets a little breathlessly as he stumbles into the diner.

"Uh, hey, Hudson," Jesse gives him a confused look from behind the corner. "Isn't it, um, a little early for lunch?"

"Didn't have breakfast," Hudson chokes out, chest heaving. "Shouldn't be on break. Got too hungry. Need hash browns. Stat."

Jesse grins as he goes to switch on the grill. "Coming right up."

⊠

"Damn, those were good," Hudson mumbles to himself as he finishes off Jesse's hashbrowns. He casts a furtive glance around the street. On finding that there's no one in particular to observe him, with all the pedestrians engrossed in their own business as they make their own way down the road, he licks his fingers, attempting to glean the last remnants of flavour from them.

"Finger lickin' good, huh?"

Hudson almost trips off the sidewalk and into the road in surprise. "Piper," he manages, before clearing his throat and crumpling the now hash-brown-less brown paper bag into one fist. "Um, hi," he says, feeling the tips of his ears begin to warm up. "What are you..."

"Coffee break," she says, holding up a paper cup emblazoned with the green Starbucks logo.

"Oh," Hudson says, a thought occurring to him. "Don't you have, like, assistants? To do that for you?" he asks as they make their way down the street.

Piper's eyes narrow. "And what makes you say that?"

Hudson shifts uncomfortably, realising his mistake. "Beth kinda told me what you do," he admits after a few moments.

"I see," she replies. "And what led to that conversation?"

He tries to shrug nonchalantly. "I may have asked about you."

"Asked about me?"

"Well, yeah," Hudson can feel the defensiveness begin to seep into his tone. "I knew pretty much nothing about you but I had a pretty good view of your entire sitting room."

Piper purses her lips. "I do have them."

"Huh?"

"Assistants," she clarifies, rolling her eyes. "But I prefer to go get my own coffee. My life isn't a carbon copy of The Devil Wears Prada."

"Right," Hudson nods. "I get it."

"Do you?" she arches an eyebrow.

"Well, I don't get it get it," he concedes, "but I get where you're coming from."

"Don't you have some doors to be knocking at?" she changes the subject, bringing her coffee cup to her lips.

"I'm on a pit stop," he says. "I forgot to have breakfast."

"I didn't know it was possible for one to forget to have breakfast," Piper snorts.

"Okay, well, I didn't have time for breakfast," Hudson corrects. "Technically, I shouldn't even be on a break."

She shrugs. "Same here."

"Can't you just give yourself breaks?"

Piper rolls her eyes again. "Yes. But that means that no work would end up getting done. And even head editors are fired sometimes."

There's something about her tone that makes Hudson feel stupid for asking. "Right," he agrees. He pauses, before adding: "I think it's really cool. What you do, I mean."

The corners of Piper's mouth turn up, and it sets off a flutter of butterflies in his stomach. "Thank you. Your job isn't too bad, either."

He smiles, maybe a little too widely, but he doesn't care. He likes Piper. He really likes Piper.

"I should probably be getting back," she juts a thumb in the opposite direction. "Might run into you at the diner, hm?"

The smile on his face grows impossibly wider. "Yeah. Definitely."

Then she goes, before it can occur to Hudson to ask if she walked past her workplace to keep up a conversation with him.

☒

"Hi sir, madam - I work for a charity called Man's Best Friend: we help disabled dogs. I was wondering if you'd be interested in - "

"Donating?" the man nods eagerly. "Yeah, totally, let me go get my wallet - "

Hudson blinks in surprise. "Ah, thanks," he says to the woman still standing at the doorway.

"He really likes dogs," she says wryly by way of explanation. Hudson nods, grinning.

"Me too," he tells her.

She laughs. "I never would've guessed."

"Here!" The man has returned, clutching four fifty dollar bills in his hand. Hudson blinks, feeling his eyes widen a little bit, but doesn't comment, choosing instead to say: "Thank you so much, sir! Here's a leaflet, if you ever think about adoption or - "

"Adoption?" the man looks like he's a five year-old who's been told Christmas has come early. "Seriously? You can do that?"

Hudson suppresses a laugh. "Yep," he hands the man the leaflet and glances at the woman, whose expression mirrors Hudson's.

"Oh, wow, this is great!" the man turns to the woman. "We should totally do this!"

"We'll see, Ed," the woman pats him on the shoulder, winking surreptitiously at Hudson.

"Thank you again, sir, madam," Hudson steps away from the doorway. "Your generosity is really appreciated. Have a great day!"

"No problem, you too!"

☒

This has been such a good day, Hudson thinks to himself as he heads back to his apartment. And it actually genuinely has been. He was barely able to heave the donations bucket into the office at the end of the day, and it earned him an impressed look from his boss, which, he thinks to himself, can only mean good things.

(Read: a promotion sometime soon.)

He didn't see Piper at the diner, but figured she was probably caught up at work. Instead, he spent his lunch break with the staff, as per usual. Beth didn't hesitate to make plenty of sexual innuendos whenever Piper came up in conversation (well, Beth was usually the one who made her come up in conversation), and Jesse told Hudson all about his girlfriend, Amanda, and what it was like back in Massachusetts while he flipped burgers on the grill. Jackie teased Hudson about how it was a miracle he wasn't gaining weight with all the burgers he was having every day, and Sam shot back to Jackie that of course he wasn't gaining weight, he was running around knocking at people's doors all day every day.

And that was when Hudson realised that he'd found himself a home in New York. And since then he hasn't been able to stop smiling, so maybe that's why he's got himself a few extra donations here and there but also a few weird looks from passersby as he walks home.

☒

Piper is on her couch at her laptop when Hudson gets home, and she looks very ready to bite someone's head off. He purses his lips and watches her type away as she holds her phone to her ear with shoulder, speaking into it urgently. She looks so stressed that she doesn't even notice him, even after she finishes her phone call and flings the telephone away from her onto the other side of the couch in evident frustration.

Hudson hesitates, before grabbing a pen and marker, writing a brief message in block capitals.

BAD DAY?

He taps on the window to get her attention. She glances up and he gives her a sympathetic look. Piper exhales slightly, before turning back to her laptop. Hudson feels his stomach drop, thinking she's ignoring him, only to have her turn the screen back round, a reply typed out in large font on a Word document.

You could say that.

Hudson purses his lips again. Somehow, a part of him doesn't like seeing her upset. He turns his piece of paper over, scrawling another message.

TAKE A BREAK.

She reads it and makes a face, typing out a reply. Too much work. Not enough time.

He fishes around for another piece of paper, grabbing a notebook from the coffee table. TWENTY MINUTES WON'T KILL YOU.

It's not a good idea.

SURE IT IS. Hudson pauses, before adding, COME WITH ME. WE'LL DO SOMETHING FUN.

Piper arches an eyebrow at his message. Like what?

SHOW ME YOUR FAVORITE PLACE IN NEW YORK CITY.

Customer Type #8: The Ones Who Are Busy

"Hello, ma'am, I'm Hudson Ellis - I'm a representative of the charity Man's Best Friend. You may have heard of us?"

"Hold on a second, Trisha, it's one of those door-to-door salesmen - " the woman is clutching her phone to her ear using her shoulder in a way that reminds Hudson forcibly of Piper. Her hands are occupied with a bowl and whisk, which she's whirling through what appears to be cake mix at a dizzying speed. "Can I help you?" she asks in a tone that really means Can you leave? Hudson perseveres nonetheless.

"Um, we're a charity that helps disabled dogs - "

"You have leaflets, right?"

"Uh, yes - "

"Great," the woman looks distinctly uncomfortable in her current position, and Hudson wonders absently how the phone perched between her shoulder and her ear hasn't fallen yet. "Do you mind just leaving me one? It's just I really don't have time right now..."

It is a truth universally acknowledged that, historically, leaving houses with just leaflets makes the residents about eighty percent less likely to donate - simply because they can't be bothered to read them, or they forget to, or they tell themselves that they will and they don't.

Despite this, Hudson smiles and nods, fishing an information pack out of his bag and holding it out to her. There's an awkward moment as she tries to find enough hands to take it from him, but she does eventually, already beginning to step away from the door.

"Thank you for your time, madam," Hudson starts to say, maybe just a little bit ironically, but the door's already been shut in his face.

⊠

"Hey."

Piper has chosen a booth towards the back of the diner. Hudson decides it's acceptable to join her, considering they haven't really talked for a few days, except for the occasional wave through their windows.

"Hey Hudson," she says absently, biting at her lip as she types at her laptop. Hudson watches her for a few moments, then rolls his eyes when she doesn't look up.

"Piper," he says, covering her still frantically moving fingers with his own hands, stopping her movements and trying to ignore the shivers that are running down his spine at the contact.

Piper finally looks up, and a beat passes, before she slumps back into the leather seat, sighing and pulling a hand away from Hudson's to run it through her hair. "Sorry," she says tiredly. "Lots of work."

"I can tell," Hudson grins, trying not to be too distracted by his other hand still on hers. "But what have we said about taking breaks?"

At that, the hints of a smile begin to play at Piper's lips. She sighs again, then moves to close her laptop. Hudson immediately misses the feeling of her fingers against his. "Sorry," she says again. "How are you?"

"I'm good," he tells her as she sips at her milkshake. "Why do I get the feeling I can't say the same for you?" he adds with a wry smile.

Piper groans, taking a bite of her burger. "Don't remind me," she grumbles. "Goddamn people slacking off their work..."

"And you have to do the work that they don't," Hudson finishes with a raised eyebrow. Piper nods, mouth full.

"Basically," she says after swallowing. "But didn't we say this is a break? No talking about work."

"True," Hudson concedes. "Although I doubt anything we do could live up to our last break," he says, grinning.

Piper smiles her typical smile, the one that's only a hint of something teasing at her lips. "I agree," she replies. "That was pretty good."

"Pretty good," Hudson scoffs. "You mean fucking awesome."

She rolls her eyes. "Fucking awesome, then. Unquote."

"Don't pretend you didn't love it."

"I don't know what you're talking about."

"It was awesome."

"Eh. Average. So was the company, to be honest."

"Piper!"

"Mm?"

"That hurts. That really hurts."

"I'm so sorry, Hudson."

☒

"It's kinda late, but that'll probably make it better," Piper mumbles as they stand side by side on the subway.

"Okay," Hudson smiles. Part of him is still in awe that she even agreed to this.

She studies him for a moment, rolling her eyes. "Do you do nothing but smile?"

Despite himself, he lets his grin widen. "It's a talent."

"Clearly."

"So, where are we going?"

Piper smiles to herself, and it's a quiet affair that makes Hudson feel very much like he's intruding on something. "You'll see," she murmurs.

They stand in comfortable silence for a few minutes, and the next time the carriage lurches to a stop, Piper tugs at his sleeve. "This is us," she says.

They step out into a part of the city that Hudson hasn't seen much of before, but Piper clearly knows her way around, walking with a kind of easy, subtle confidence that only a native in their hometown could possess. He wonders absently if this is what he's like in Dallas. Unbidden, an image of him showing Piper his own favourite place back home comes into his mind. Hudson blinks, long and slow, trying to clear his mind of the thought. He barely knows Piper. This is not a good way to be thinking.

"Hudson," she turns back to raise an eyebrow at him, and he realises he's standing stock still in the middle of the sidewalk.

"Sorry," he apologises, trying to ignore the somersaults his stomach is doing at the sound of her saying his name. "I'm coming."

She rolls her eyes again - if Hudson has a talent for smiling, Piper has a talent for rolling her eyes and being just generally cynical. "Hurry up, then."

He follows her as they wind their way through several roads, each with buildings more beautiful than the last. Hudson's no architect, but he can appreciate a lovely building when he sees one. Piper smirks slightly as he stares open-mouthed at one. "They're nice, huh?" she offers, but it's all she says on the subject as they continue on their way. Hudson guesses she's been here enough times for it to lose its overall charm.

"Okay," she exhales slightly. "Here you go. My favourite place in New York."

It's not hard to see why this is Piper's favourite place. They're standing on a wide, large bridge overlooking the city. A nearby plaque attached to the railings they're leaning against reads "Brooklyn Heights Promenade". Hudson blinks at the city below him, lights shimmering as they're reflected in the water.

"It's..."

"Beautiful?" Piper finishes. "Yeah. I think so too." She pauses, before adding: "Who wouldn't?"

He studies the view for a little longer, before turning to face her. "So what's the story?"

"Story?"

"This is your favourite place. Everyone's favourite things have reasons behind them."

Piper purses her lips, seemingly in some kind of internal conflict. "My parents used to bring me here," she admits eventually.

"Used to?"

There's another pause. "We're not exactly on...good terms. Any more. With each other, I mean."

Hudson lets the words hang in the air, fixing her with a steady gaze. Piper sighs, leaning a little more against the railings. "They kicked me out," she says after a long silence, words that would be fragile if they weren't said in such a matter-of-fact tone. "Because I wanted to major in fashion at college."

Hudson watches her, profile framed against the backdrop of a city still awake at night. "Didn't stop you, though," he says softly. Piper lets out an almost-chuckle on an exhale.

"No," she says in a similar tone. "I suppose it didn't."

There's another silence, one that they're both lulled into. "Thank you for bringing me here," Hudson says eventually.

"I'm glad you appreciate it," the cynical edge has returned to Piper's voice with a vengeance. "Because now I've got double the work to do and half the time to do it in when I get home."

Hudson bites his lip to stop himself from smiling. "Worth it, though?"

She raises an eyebrow. "Semi worth it."

"Worth it."

"Three-fourths worth it."

"Worth it."

"Kind of worth it."

"Worth it."

"Almost worth it."

Customer Type #9: The Ones Who Are Sceptical

"Hello, ma'am, I'm Hudson Ellis - I'm a representative of the charity Man's Best Friend. You may have heard of us?"

"Let me guess," the woman purses her lips, shifting her weight onto one leg and resting a hand on her hip. "You help dogs. And you want me to donate."

"Well, yes," Hudson agrees, trying his hardest not to smile.

She raises an eyebrow at his bluntness. "And why should I do that?"

This woman, thinks Hudson to himself, is too much like Piper for my tastes. And not half as attractive.

"Well, these are the types of dogs you'll be helping," Hudson already has a flyer ready, showing it to her. "And they'd really appreciate it."

"They're dogs."

"Dogs can show appreciation too," Hudson tells her, trying to keep the offended tone from glancing off his voice. "Haven't you ever seen a happy dog with its owner?"

The woman's eyes soften. Hudson congratulates himself on finding a chink in the metaphorical armour. "Well, yeah," she concedes in a far milder tone than before.

"Well, maybe you should consider it," he suggests, holding out the flyer to her hesitantly. She stares at it for a moment, indecision flickering over her face, before bringing her fingers out to skim the glossy paper and taking it from Hudson's hand.

"I'm not making any promises," she warns.

"Of course," Hudson acknowledges with a nod and barely suppressed smile. "But thank you anyway, Miss."

⊠

Hudson makes the decision to go back home for his lunch break when he realises his final customer isn't that far way from his apartment. To his surprise, Piper is lounging on her own couch in front of the television with a bowl of popcorn, hair down and wearing sweatpants and a baggy tee.

This is ridiculous, Hudson thinks to himself, trying his best not to stare. No one should look that good in sweatpants. It shouldn't be legal.

After some time, he figures he might as well say hi, and thuds on the window with his fist. Piper turns, caught off guard, then sees him, and the surprise in her expression only becomes more pronounced - she skids off the couch and lands hard on her backside, bowl of popcorn following suit. Miraculously, the majority of the popcorn has managed to stay intact (and in the bowl), although Hudson has a feeling Piper's pride has not. He watches her lower her head into her hands, and his stomach immediately plummets.

Oh shit. This is where she flips me off and files a restraining order. And decides to move apartments. Possibly apartment blocks.

It's a completely backwards way of thinking that both Hudson and Piper will later both come to renounce and laugh about for quite a long time afterwards, but at this moment in time, it seems very real to Hudson as he watches Piper slumped over a bowl of popcorn on her living room floor with her hands covering her face from view.

Timidly, he moves forwards, tapping at the glass again, almost questioningly. Piper looks up.

Her whole body is vibrating with silent laughter.

Hudson sighs in relief.

A few moments pass, and she reaches for a pen and paper. YOU SCARED ME.

He grins. Sorry, he mouths, though he doubts he looks very sorry at all. Piper catching him off guard is a regular occurrence. Him catching Piper off guard, however, is an extremely rare event, and Hudson thinks it should be celebrated as such.

DAY OFF, she scrawls onto the other side of the paper, holding it up and making an all-encompassing gesture towards her clothing with her other hand. Hudson gives her a knowing smirk that clearly says I taught you well.

It's been almost four months since Piper showed Hudson her favourite place in New York City, and he's currently coming to the conclusion that, cheesy and ridiculous as it sounds, his favourite place is…with her.

At the end of the day, they're pretty much roommates with a slab of glass in between them – Hudson's seen Piper before she's done her hair in the morning, witnessed her fall over in high heels (something he still finds hilarious, considering she wears them pretty much every day), seen her work on private portfolios of designs that are so beautiful they leave him winded, watched her yell into her cell and at her cell and also at her wall, watched her throw her cell at her wall, and it's okay, because she's probably seen him do some equally crazy shit through the window of their living area too.

Meeting up for lunch happens at least twice a week now, and he's realised that Piper makes pretty much his shittiest days better just by being sarcastic and cynical and Piper.

And he realises as he watches her pick stray pieces of popcorn from the carpet and slide back onto the couch with a slightly sardonic double thumbs-up that he should probably get round to asking her out because that's something he really wants to do.

⊠

"Hello," Hudson says brightly, having to bend his neck slightly to look at his newest potential customer. "Is there a grown-up here I can talk to?"

"Mommy's at work and Daddy's shopping," the small girl informs him stiffly, crossing her arms. "You can talk to me about it."

Hudson shrugs inwardly, figuring he might as well. "We help disabled dogs," he explains, crouching down to meet her eyes. He watches them narrow.

"How?"

"Well," Hudson begins slowly. "Say if they've lost a leg. We try and train them to walk with just three."

"Dogs are smart," she points out. "They can teach themselves."

"True," he admits. She's tough. "But we wanna help them out a bit. Plus, we can give them food and water and somewhere to live while we're at it."

"Okay," the girl says. "How do I know you're actually from a charity and not just a random man? What if you're trying to kidnap me?"

"If I wanted to kidnap you, I would have done it by now."

She blinks. "Fine. But I don't have any money to give you."

"Ava!" A rather ruffled man hurtles towards the door, looking concerned. "What have we said about opening the door while your mother and I are out? And talking to strangers?"

"He's not a stranger. He helps disabled dogs," Ava informs her father seriously. "And I know his name. It's – " she pauses to squint at Hudson's name tag. "Hud. Son. Hudsun."

"Sorry, sir," Hudson thinks it's a good time to cut in, before things get too out of hand and Ava mentions the conversation they've just had about Hudson being a potential kidnapper. "Your daughter and I were just talking about the charity I work for."

"It looks okay," Ava says reasonably. "But it might be a waste of money if you donate because Hudsun said that they help dogs with three legs to walk but most dogs with three legs can probably teach themselves."

The man raises an eyebrow at his daughter. "Thanks for the advice, Ava."

"What's advice?"

"Okay, how much do you want?" The man asks, giving Hudson's bucket a glance as he does so.

"Any donations are appreciated, sir," Hudson recites, smiling.

"Daddy! Is that the money you were going to buy my new toy with?" Ava brings out a small hand to stop her father's own, which is bearing a five dollar bill.

"No, Ava," the man says patiently. "This is different money."

"If you give the Different Money to Hudsun does that mean I don't get my toy?"

"Nope. You'll still get it."

Ava considers this for a moment, face screwed up in concentration. "Okay. I guess you could give him some Different Money, then."

⊠

"And that was my day," Hudson finishes. Georgie is leaning into his shoulder as they both sit on the couch (her body taking up three quarters of the space, seeing as she's completely stretched out onto it. Both of them are watching the conclusion of another episode of Friends (which they both know every episode of off by heart, and therefore aren't paying very much attention to).

"Sounds fascinating," Georgie manages through a yawn, moving slightly away from Hudson to stretch herself out before slumping back into his lap.

"No need for the sarcasm," he tells her, flicking her cheek with his fingernail. "I doubt your day was much better."

"You're right," she muses. "It was mostly filled with a lot of dickheads with their dickish books about dickish things being dickish enough to think they can get published."

"That's a lot of dick," he replies. "You and Piper would get along very well."

"Oh yeah, she's an editor too, isn't she?" Georgie remembers.

"Mhm," he hums in affirmation.

"I need to meet her," she says.

"Okay," Hudson says, stifling a yawn. "We'll work something out."

"We better," she warns him. "I'm interested to see the woman who's stolen my best friend's heart."

Hudson rolls his eyes. "She hasn't stolen – "

"Stop right there, Hudson Ellis," Georgie reaches up to press her hand to his mouth. "She has totally stolen your heart. You are fucking whipped."

"Okay," he admits. "Maybe I am a little bit."

---

a/n: fun fact: here in england we spell sceptical w/ a "c" plz dont bitch me out for it bc i will bitch u out back and i am most likely bitchier than u

Customer Type #10: The Ones Who Want The Details

"Hello, ma'am, I'm Hudson Ellis - I'm a representative of the charity Man's Best Friend. You may have heard of us?"

Piper rolls her eyes, but it's almost pointless considering the small smile playing on her lips. "Shut up, Hudson."

"I have the boxset," he informs her gravely, holding up the aforementioned collection.

"And I have the popcorn," she replies in just as similar a tone. They stare at each other intently for a moment, before Hudson breaks out into a wide grin. "Let's watch Game of Thrones!" he exclaims brightly.

Piper rolls her eyes, but moves for him to come inside.

"Nice flat," Hudson compliments, flopping down onto the couch after taking off his shoes at the door.

"Like you haven't seen the inside of it before," Piper retorts, taking the boxset from where he's left it on the coffee table and kneeling to put the first disc into the player.

"Well, not properly," he says, concentrating on looking around him and not Piper because she's kneeling down and not facing him and they all know what that means.

"Uh, yes, properly," she turns around, having pressed play, and heads back to the couch. "Those floor-to-ceiling windows don't leave much to the imagination," she teases, elbowing him in the stomach.

"Ouch," Hudson rubs the injured part of his body with a pout. "Okay, that's true. I can't believe the landlord won't let us put curtains up just because he doesn't want holes drilled into the wall."

"Eh, I don't know, I quite like it," Piper says lightly, reaching for the remote whilst grabbing a handful of popcorn (the sure sign of a veteran TV marathoner). Hudson tries his best to stop his heart from skipping too many beats, and shoves popcorn into his mouth to stop himself from saying anything, because he doesn't really trust himself to do that without something stupid being the result.

☒

"Daenerys is such a badass," Piper says around halfway through the first episode. Hudson hums in agreement.

"She's really hot, too," he sighs. Piper elbows him in the stomach yet again, and he lets out a squeal in protest.

"What was that for?" he whines.

"For objectifying her," she retorts without removing her eyes from the screen.

"I was not!" he denies. "I was just pointing out how beautiful the genes of her parents came together to make her! I was appreciating the wonders of biology!"

"Whatever, Hudson."

☒

"Can't look," Hudson declares, covering his eyes as yet another maiming takes place onscreen.

"Wimp," Piper mutters.

"Is it over?" he asks meekly, ignoring her comment and peeking throught the gaps between his fingers. He can practically hear Piper rolling her eyes.

"Yeah. You can look."

Hudson lets out a sigh of relief. "Jeez, I hate that stuff."

"Really?" Piper asks with mock-interest. "I never would have guessed."

Hudson, lacking a suitable comeback, chooses instead to stick his tongue out at her. She snorts. "Real mature of you, Hudson," she tells him.

Hudson sniffs. "Maturity iwould be lost on you, anyway."

"Is that so?" Piper arches a brow, and Hudson resists the urge to shout please don't do that because it's really sexy and it makes me want to jump your bones literally right here in the middle of your living room.

"Yes, it's so," he manages to choke out.

"Just watch the show. We've missed like half of the Daenerys scene already."

"You've already seen it!"

"You can never have enough of strong, powerful female leads, Hudson."

You're telling me, Hudson bites back, because Piper Henderson is pretty much the strong, powerful female lead in the pathetic comedy that is his life.

☒

"Joffrey is such a dick."

"Agreed."

☒

It's only after three more episodes that Hudson instils enough courage into himself to even think about doing what he's desperately wanted to do since very possibly the Piper Henderson first slammed her apartment door in his face.

Hudson waits till Daenerys has made her exit, then clears his throat. "Um, Piper," he manages, feeling his voice waver. She turns to look at him. He clears his throat again, before clenching his fists, hoping that the action will somehow dispel the butterflies in his stomach.

(It does no such thing.)

"I've been - uh, I kinda wanted to ask - um..."

Piper cocks her head to the side, raising her eyebrows. Hudson feels himself getting flashbacks to that very first day, the sarcastic I'm very sorry and the slamming of doors.

"Ifmaybeyou'dwanttogoonadatewithme," he forces out, the words crashing into each other. "Some time. Like, uh...together. For dinner, or - or - " Hudson can feel himself floundering, but Piper isn't exactly offering him any support. Her brow is furrowed in a frown, and it's with that look that he realises that him and Piper aren't going anywhere together - not on a date, at any rate.

"I don't think that's going to work out, Hudson," she murmurs softly, not looking at him, and Hudson feels like he's just been punched directly in the stomach.

"Oh," he breathes out. "Okay."

It's not okay, it's very far from okay, probably as far from okay as physically possible, but it's not like Hudson can do much about it, except perhaps escape with the remnants of his dignity and try and piece it back together slowly in his bedroom, alone, where there are no floor-to-ceiling windows.

So he does.

⊠

"Okay," Georgie announces, bursting into the bedroom. "I'm here. And I've brought reinforcements."

"What?" Hudson says blearily, sitting up. Jesse and Beth poke their heads into the doorway with smiles caught halfway between sympathy and blinding optimism.

"We're going to make you the best dinner ever," Jesse informs him.

⊠

"...she just said it wouldn't work out," Hudson mumbles through what is genuinely the best dinner ever.

"Did she say why?" Georgie asks, thoughtful.

"No," he replies miserably, pushing his food around his plate with his fork. Suddenly, the best dinner ever doesn't seem so appetising any more.

"Well, here's how I see it," Beth says round a forkful of the best dinner ever. "There are a few possible reasons she could have turned you down. One. She's not a head editor of anything, and is actually a criminal on the run from the government. Two. She's a Canadian immigrant and she's about to be deported."

"That sounds a little too much like the plot of The Proposal for my liking," Georgie says doubtfully. Jesse hums in agreement.

"Ssh, I'm not done. Three. She's a lesbian. Four. She's a hologram and not a real person."

Hudson blinks. "Or," he says slowly. "She just doesn't like me."

Immediately, all three of his friends make sounds of fervent disapproval.

"No way, bro."

"Don't be stupid."

"For fuck's sake, Hudson!"

"What do you mean, don't be stupid!" Hudson declares angrily, flinging his fork onto the table. "She said no! Most people take that as an I don't like you that way!"

"Hudson," Georgie says calmly. "If she didn't like you that way, she would not have allowed you a large and lavish view into her apartment for the past six months."

"Then what?" Hudson demands.

Beth shrugs. "Can't really explain how Piper's mind works. You're the only one who could really do that."

"Piper's a pretty lonely person," Jesse adds quietly. "You're one of her only friends."

Despite himself, Hudson wonders how someone as unreal as Piper can not have friends.

☒

"Hi, sir, would you like to donate to our charity?" Hudson asks in a monotone. His boss has noticed that he's been bringing back a lot fewer donations in the past few days. Hudson can't bring himself to care.

"Well, what do you do?"

"Disabled dogs. We help disabled dogs."

The man raises an eyebrow. "And how will my money help a disabled dog?"

"Well, sir, we do a variety of different things to help a dog," Hudson explains, trying to keep exhaustion from tinging his voice and taking out a flyer, holding it out to the man.

He looks it over, frowning. "Here," he points to a word on the piece of paper. "What do you mean by..."

Hudson sighs.

☒

It's been two weeks, and he hasn't seen Piper at all - not at the diner, and not even from the window of his apartment. Half of him worries, and the other half hates himself for worrying, because he shouldn't, he shouldn't care this much about Piper any more, she obviously doesn't care about him, right?

Hudson knows that this isn't true, that it's a childish way of thinking, that just because Piper turned him down doesn't mean that she doesn't care about him, but it still hurts to think about, the sound of her voice, gentle and low like chocolate, playing the same words over and over: I don't think that's going to work out, Hudson, I don't think that's going to work out, Hudson, I don't think that's going to work out, Hudson, I don't think that's going to work out, Hudson, and yeah, that hurts, but it's not enough for Hudson to stop glancing every night at his window.

☒

"So, this sponsoring system - what do I..."

"The information's on the leaflet, Miss," he gestures to the piece of folded paper he's already placed in her hands, reaching over to point out the section on sponsoring.

"Ah, I see," the woman nods. "So, when I do this, is it..."

Hudson thinks he's staring too long at her face, because somehow every time he blinks he sees Piper's instead. The woman's hair is the exact same colour as Piper's, and it's distracting him from what she's actually saying. He feels a little dizzy.

"Um, excuse me?"

Hudson shakes his head, attempting to jerk himself out of his trance and offering the woman a concilatory smile. "Sorry," he says. "Say that again?"

☒

"Hudson," Georgie says, giving a long-suffering sigh. "You can't stay in bed forever."

"I can," he mumbles from underneath his comforter (which is drawn up and over his head). "And I will."

"No, you won't," she replies with a tone of finality in her voice, and before he knows it, she's pulled the blanket completely off of him.

"Cold," he exclaims, bringing his arms to wrap around his body.

"No pain, no gain," Georgie says with not one hint of sympathy in her voice, crossing the room to wrench open the curtains.

"Sunlight," Hudson moans, moving his arms from his body to his eyes.

"And what a beautiful sun it is," Georgie sighs in mock-happiness. "A disc of white light in the crisp blue sky, shimmering over the world."

"Was that the opening of another book you looked at today?" Hudson mumbles, eyes slowly adjusting to the light.

"Yep," Georgie says, beginning to exit the room.

"Did you reject it?"

"Hudson," she scoffs. "The author describes the sun as a disc of white light. What do you think?"

☒

"...and you also have the option to adopt a dog."

"Oh, wow, that sounds great, doesn't it, Bobby?" the woman smiles down at her son, who nods his head eagerly. "If you could just explain to us one more time what this involves..."

I could. But I just, Hudson thinks to himself as his mouth says completely different things. Want Piper back.

☒

When his doorbell rings, Hudson can barely heave himself off the couch and to the front door, and even then, there's a lot of internal debate as to whether he can even be bothered to talk to another human being. Realising it could possibly be Georgie or, failing that, Jesse or Beth, he twists the doorknob and lets the door swing open.

And now he isn't sure whether he regrets opening it or not.

"Hi," Piper says.

"Hi," Hudson parrots back to her, and he realises that he sounds completely wrecked, and he supposes that's what she's done to him.

"I, uh, I came to talk."

"It's been a month," he says in a monotone.

Piper lets her eyes drop to the floor. "I know," she says quietly. "But you deserve an explanation as to why...well, why I turned you down." There's a pause. "And you didn't exactly give me a chance to do that at the time," she adds, perhaps a tad wryly, except Hudson can't really tell, because she's still practically talking to the floor.

"Okay," he manages. At this, Piper looks up, studies his face for a moment, then takes a deep breath, expelling it all in one go.

"Okay," she says. There's a pause, before she takes another breath. "Three months ago, I was offered a new job. In California."

Hudson blinks.

"And because I'm sad and I don't have friends and I'm a loner and I barely had any friends in my own hometown with the small exception of the waiting staff who served me my lunch every other day, I took it, because I told myself that I wouldn't have much to lose."

She stops here, not looking at him. He doesn't say anything, silently urging her to continue.

"Three months ago, I didn't know you all that well," Piper admits, voice slightly shaky. "Sure, we'd wave at each other once in a while, maybe say hi if we ran into each other, but it wasn't much. I figured if I had nothing to lose, and no one else did either, then I might as well go."

"Then..." she trails off. "Then, you happened," she lets out a quiet laugh. "And you talked to me and sat with me and no matter how hard I tried to make you, you didn't go away. And we did the notes at our window thing and sometimes we'd sit and watch the same TV show on each other's televisions through each other's windows and I..." she runs a hand through her hair and looks up at him for the first time. Hudson feels shivers run down his spine. "I showed you my favourite place," she murmurs softly.

"So, because I sound like something straight out of a romantic comedy or possibly just a cheesy romance with a pathetically cliche ending that at the moment I doubt I'm actually going to get, I'm going to finish up. I realised too late that I had something to lose," Piper admits. "And I realised too late that for you, I was something to lose. And when I told you that it wasn't going to work out, I believed it. Because I always screw things up when there's something to lose."

Hudson looks at her for a moment, then takes a step closer. "You never screw things up," he mutters stupidly, looking down at her. "You're Piper."

She exhales. "I..."

"When's your flight?" he murmurs.

"If my calculations are correct, it took off approximately ten minutes ago."

Hudson bites his lip to keep a silly grin from spreading across his face, before moving his forehead to bump with hers. "See," he says softly. "You never screw things up."

"Are you planning on kissing me?"

"Maybe. It depends on whether you'll kiss me back."

"That's not something I'm going to inform you of," she tells him lowly. "You're just going to take a chance."

Hudson does grin this time, moving his hands to cup her cheeks. "I did that the first time, and look where it got me."

"Shut up," she whispers, and then she's pressing her lips to his and she kisses like Piper would, with enough force to make him take a few steps back but enough softness to let the word finally resonate in the back of his brain.

"This - this is some form of - poetic justice," she mutters against his lips in between kisses.

"Oh?" Hudson asks.

"Mm," she confirms, lips falling on his again.

"And why is that?"

Piper smirks, her signature smirk that is gorgeous and reckless and one that Hudson finally knows the taste of. "Don't you do all your best work on a doorstep?"

CPSIA information can be obtained
at www.ICGtesting.com
Printed in the USA
LVHW041237030123
736313LV00011B/1001

9 781837 616022